Published by Advance Publishers, L.C.
Maitland, FL 32751 USA
www.advancepublishers.com
Produced by Judy O Productions, Inc.
Designed by SunDried Penguin
© 2006 Disney Enterprises, Inc.
Stitch! The Movie
Printed in the United States of America

One day, Lilo taught her alien friend, Stitch, to say, "Aloha cousin" to the people on the beach. But everyone was scared of Stitch and ran away. That night, Stitch looked in the mirror, and felt sad that he didn't have any cousins that were like him. Lilo told him he was part of her ohana, her family. She knew how hard it can be to make friends when you are different.

That night, Lilo's sister, Nani, went out and left the aliens, Pleakley and Jumba, to look after Lilo and Stitch. Suddenly, there was a crash outside! It was the evil alien Captain Gantu in his spaceship. He had been sent by Jumba's old partner, Dr Hamsterviel, to kidnap Jumba and the alien experiments he'd been secretly working on.

Jumba hid Pleakley and his experiments in a toy box, but Experiment 625 fell out and rolled away. Just then, Gantu pulled the roof off and grabbed Jumba. Jumba wouldn't tell him where the experiments were, but Gantu saw 625 on the floor. He grabbed Jumba and 625, and set off in his ship.

Lilo and Stitch tried to follow, but lost them. When they got home, Lilo told Nani what had happened and she called their old friend, Agent Cobra Bubbles, to ask for help. When Stitch found Pleakley and the experiments in the toy box, Pleakley told them that if the experiments got wet they'd come to life and cause trouble. Then Pleakley used his alien phone to ring around the galaxy to look for Jumba.

Naughty Lilo and Stitch put one of Jumba's experiments in the bath to see what would happen. As soon as Experiment 221 hit the water, it exploded into life in a shower of sparks and blew all the lights in the house, before jumping out the window.

Gantu arrived at Dr Hamsterviel's lair with Jumba and 625. Jumba wouldn't tell them where the experiments were, so Hamsterviel dropped 625 into water – and he came to life! But he wasn't scary at all! "Funny thing," laughed Jumba, "625 has all the powers of 626, but he is also a lazy coward – he makes great sandwiches, though!"

Pleakley finally got in touch with Jumba on his alien phone. But Dr Hamsterviel took the phone and said, if they ever wanted to see Jumba again they had to give him all the experiments. He said he'd call Pleakley later to tell them where to meet him.

The next day, Cobra Bubbles came to help and they waited for Dr Hamsterviel's call. Lilo and Stitch stole Cobra's car and went off to search the island for 221. They caught him in a glass vase and took him back to Stitch's room. Stitch realized 221 was just like him, his ohana, and Stitch told Lilo he didn't want to send 221 away.

Dr Hamsterviel called and said to meet him at the lighthouse. He and Gantu arrived with Jumba but, before they set him free, Dr Hamsterviel realized Experiment 221 was missing. He was very angry. Lilo and Stitch arrived just in time with the missing 221, who Lilo had named Sparky. But she refused to hand him over. "I've got to save Sparky, too!" Lilo cried, and set 221 free while Stitch rescued Jumba.

Suddenly, a spaceship rose out of the sea – it was the Grand Councilwoman of Stitch's planet, Turo. Cobra had told her she'd be able to catch Dr Hamsterviel and Gantu there. She pointed her ship's guns at Dr Hamsterviel and the experiments, but Stitch and 221 used their special powers to stop the guns from firing.

Dr Hamsterviel escaped with the experiments but Lilo, Stitch and 221 snuck on board his ship. Stitch grabbed the experiments and Lilo threw them to safety out one of the windows. Then, just as Dr Hamsterviel caught Stitch and trapped Lilo, 221 saved the day by helping Stitch escape – and then Stitch rescued Lilo.

When they got back to Earth, Dr Hamsterviel was caught and 221 was rewarded with the job of lighting the lighthouse. Then the Grand Councilwoman put Lilo and Stitch in charge of finding all the lost experiments. "C'mon!" said Lilo to Stitch. "We've got cousins to find!"

The End